Herb, The Vegetarian Dragon

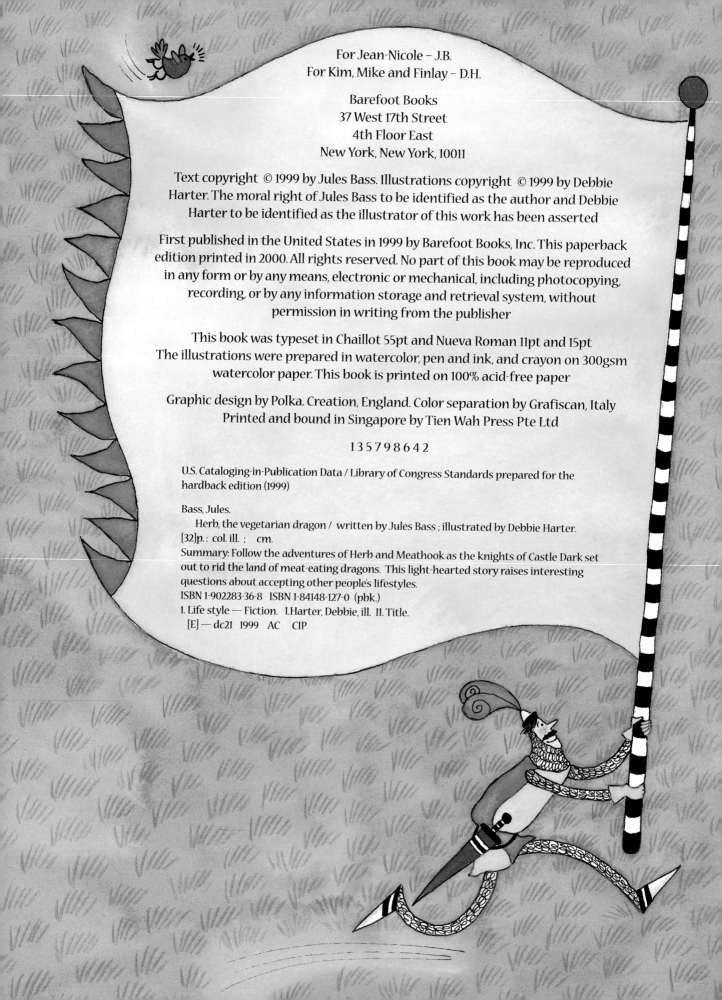

For Jean-Nicole – J.B.
For Kim, Mike and Finlay – D.H.

Barefoot Books
37 West 17th Street
4th Floor East
New York, New York, 10011

This book was typeset in Chaillot 55pt and Nueva Roman 11pt and 15pt
The illustrations were prepared in watercolor, pen and ink, and crayon on 300gsm watercolor paper. This book is printed on 100% acid-free paper

Graphic design by Polka. Creation, England. Color separation by Grafiscan, Italy
Printed and bound in Singapore by Tien Wah Press Pte Ltd

1 3 5 7 9 8 6 4 2

U.S. Cataloging-in-Publication Data / Library of Congress Standards prepared for the hardback edition (1999)

Bass, Jules.
    Herb, the vegetarian dragon / written by Jules Bass ; illustrated by Debbie Harter.
[32]p. : col. ill. ;   cm.
Summary: Follow the adventures of Herb and Meathook as the knights of Castle Dark set out to rid the land of meat-eating dragons. This light-hearted story raises interesting questions about accepting other people's lifestyles.
ISBN 1-902283-36-8   ISBN 1-84148-127-0 (pbk.)
1. Life style — Fiction. I.Harter, Debbie, ill. II. Title.
   [E] — dc21 1999 AC   CIP

Herb, The Vegetarian Dragon

written by **J**ules **B**ass

illustrated by **D**ebbie **H**arter

walk
the way of wonder...

Barefoot Books

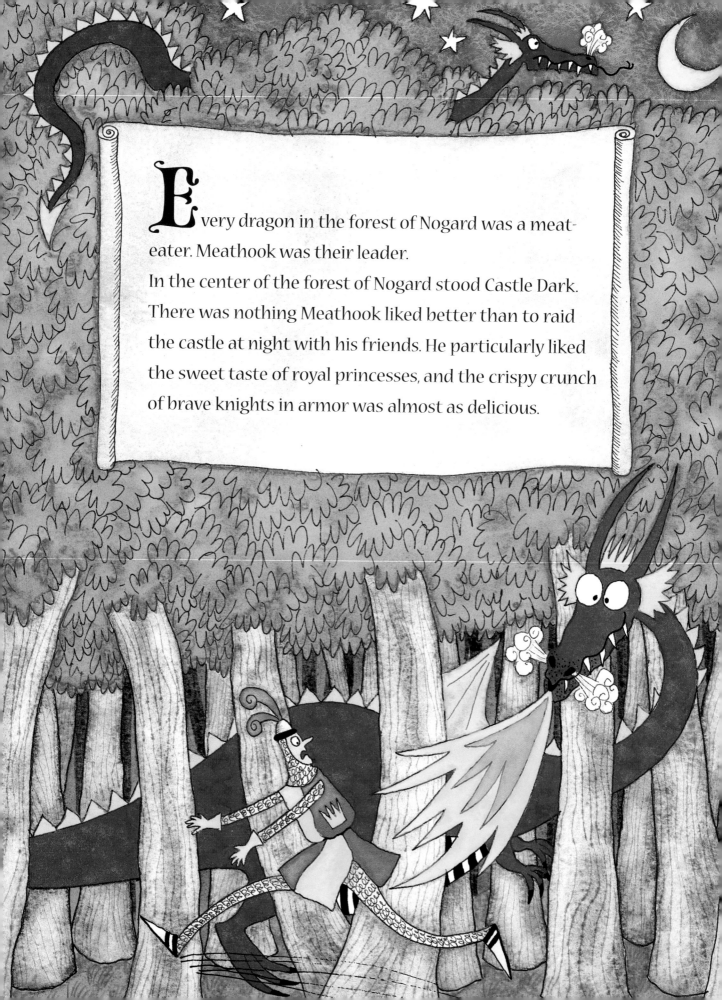

Every dragon in the forest of Nogard was a meat-eater. Meathook was their leader.

In the center of the forest of Nogard stood Castle Dark. There was nothing Meathook liked better than to raid the castle at night with his friends. He particularly liked the sweet taste of royal princesses, and the crispy crunch of brave knights in armor was almost as delicious.

But one dragon was different. While Meathook and his friends sat in his cave planning their next raid, Herb was happy to tend his vegetable patch. Sometimes, a little girl came to watch him. He grew turnips and tomatoes, leeks and lettuce, cauliflowers and carrots. He grew peas and parsnips, red and yellow peppers, potatoes and parsley. For Herb was a vegetarian.

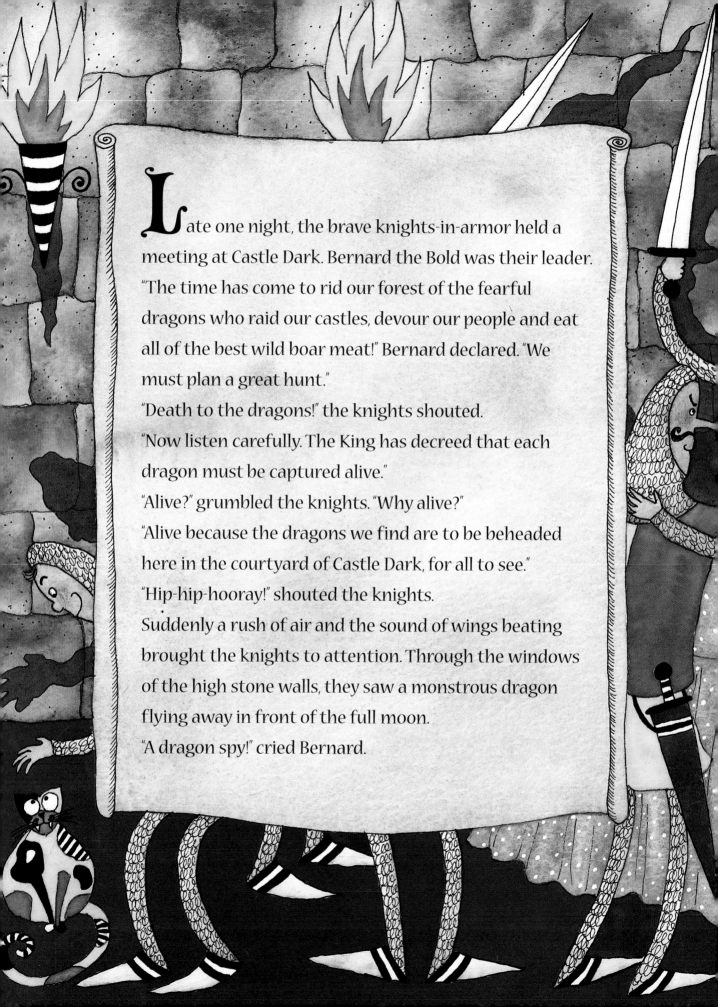

Late one night, the brave knights-in-armor held a meeting at Castle Dark. Bernard the Bold was their leader.

"The time has come to rid our forest of the fearful dragons who raid our castles, devour our people and eat all of the best wild boar meat!" Bernard declared. "We must plan a great hunt."

"Death to the dragons!" the knights shouted.

"Now listen carefully. The King has decreed that each dragon must be captured alive."

"Alive?" grumbled the knights. "Why alive?"

"Alive because the dragons we find are to be beheaded here in the courtyard of Castle Dark, for all to see."

"Hip-hip-hooray!" shouted the knights.

Suddenly a rush of air and the sound of wings beating brought the knights to attention. Through the windows of the high stone walls, they saw a monstrous dragon flying away in front of the full moon.

"A dragon spy!" cried Bernard.

The dragons met in a huge, hidden cave. Herb, who had not been invited, knew nothing of the knights' scheme.

Meathook spoke:

"My friends, the knights are planning a hunt. We'll be ready for them, won't we?"

And in answer, dragon tails pounded the earthen floor and the cave shook with the sound of thundering, evil voices:

"We'll singe 'em, fry 'em,

Boil 'em in a pot;

Stew 'em, steam 'em,

The whole juicy lot!"

"NO!" bellowed Meathook. "We shall disappear. Stay hidden in our caves. Wait them out. Then, we shall attack! And then you can sing your songs!"

The dragons roared their approval of his plan, and their fiery tongues lashed the roof of the huge cave.

As this was happening, Herb was cooking a new soup made of butter, leeks, onions and potatoes. "Mmmm," he smiled, licking his lips. "Very tasty. I must give it a name — 'Herb's Famous Lakewater Veggie Slurp'."

Herb didn't realize that he was in danger; that when the knights set out, he would be the only dragon to be seen in all of Nogard forest.

That evening a hundred knights, in groups of four, set forth on their hunt, each heading in a different direction. For seven days and seven nights they searched, but not a dragon was to be seen.

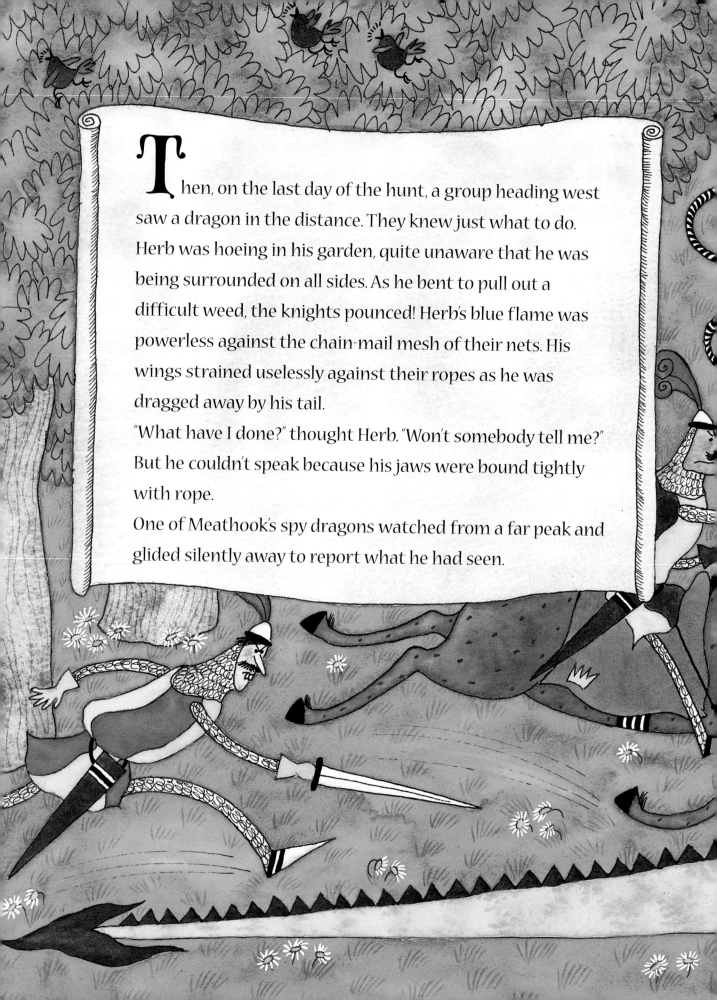

Then, on the last day of the hunt, a group heading west saw a dragon in the distance. They knew just what to do. Herb was hoeing in his garden, quite unaware that he was being surrounded on all sides. As he bent to pull out a difficult weed, the knights pounced! Herb's blue flame was powerless against the chain-mail mesh of their nets. His wings strained uselessly against their ropes as he was dragged away by his tail.

"What have I done?" thought Herb. "Won't somebody tell me?" But he couldn't speak because his jaws were bound tightly with rope.

One of Meathook's spy dragons watched from a far peak and glided silently away to report what he had seen.

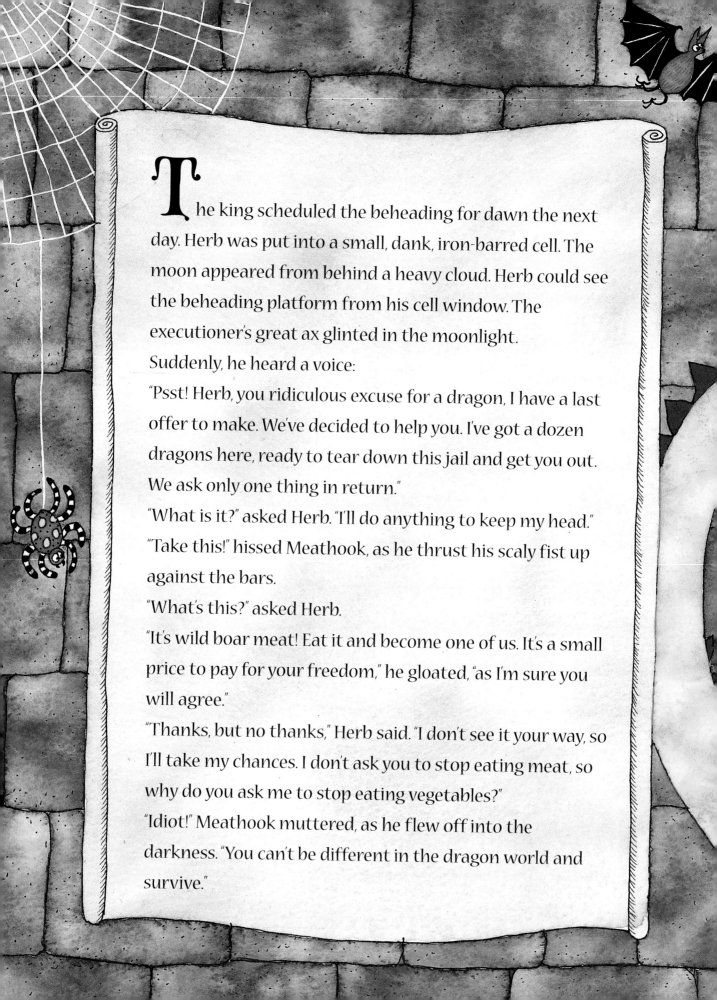

The king scheduled the beheading for dawn the next day. Herb was put into a small, dank, iron-barred cell. The moon appeared from behind a heavy cloud. Herb could see the beheading platform from his cell window. The executioner's great ax glinted in the moonlight. Suddenly, he heard a voice:

"Psst! Herb, you ridiculous excuse for a dragon, I have a last offer to make. We've decided to help you. I've got a dozen dragons here, ready to tear down this jail and get you out. We ask only one thing in return."

"What is it?" asked Herb. "I'll do anything to keep my head."

"Take this!" hissed Meathook, as he thrust his scaly fist up against the bars.

"What's this?" asked Herb.

"It's wild boar meat! Eat it and become one of us. It's a small price to pay for your freedom," he gloated, "as I'm sure you will agree."

"Thanks, but no thanks," Herb said. "I don't see it your way, so I'll take my chances. I don't ask you to stop eating meat, so why do you ask me to stop eating vegetables?"

"Idiot!" Meathook muttered, as he flew off into the darkness. "You can't be different in the dragon world and survive."

Thousands of people crowded into the square as Herb was dragged from his cell toward the beheading platform. His head was placed on a wooden block and his wings and feet secured with iron shackles. A rope held his jaws shut.

A huge, black-hooded man picked up the ax and stepped forward:

"For the crimes of burning, stealing and murdering, and to serve as an example for all who would dare to repeat these actions, this evil dragon's head will be stuffed and placed on the castle gates for all to behold."

The crowd roared its approval. A drummer rolled his sticks as the executioner raised his ax.

At that moment, with only one single second of Herb's life left, a tiny voice cried out:

"WAIT!"

The drumming stopped. The executioner held his ax in mid-swing. All heads turned to see a little girl running up the stairs of the platform.

"This dragon is my friend. His name is Herb. I have watched him tend his vegetable patch. I have played with him and never once has he tried to harm me. He only eats vegetables. You must spare his life!"

"Stop!" cried Bernard the Bold, as he moved toward the girl. "How do we know what you say is true?"

The little girl walked slowly around Herb, until she was standing in front of his huge snout. Before anyone could stop her, she released the end of the rope that held his jaws closed and they snapped open, with a rush of blue flame.

"Nicole, get down from there!" shouted a man.

"It's all right, Father," said Nicole. Then she climbed right into Herb's mouth and sat there, with only her legs dangling free. Herb gulped and tried to smile.

"See? Now do you believe me?" cried Nicole. "He wouldn't harm anyone."

As the awestruck crowd stared up at her, the silence was broken by a loud crash. Meathook, who was spying on the execution, had fallen out of his treetop hiding place. He lay helpless on the ground, his wings entangled in a mass of branches. At once, twelve knights sprang forward and bound him with ropes.

"That's one of the meat-eaters!" shouted the little girl, as she climbed out of Herb's mouth.

"Behead them both!" someone yelled.

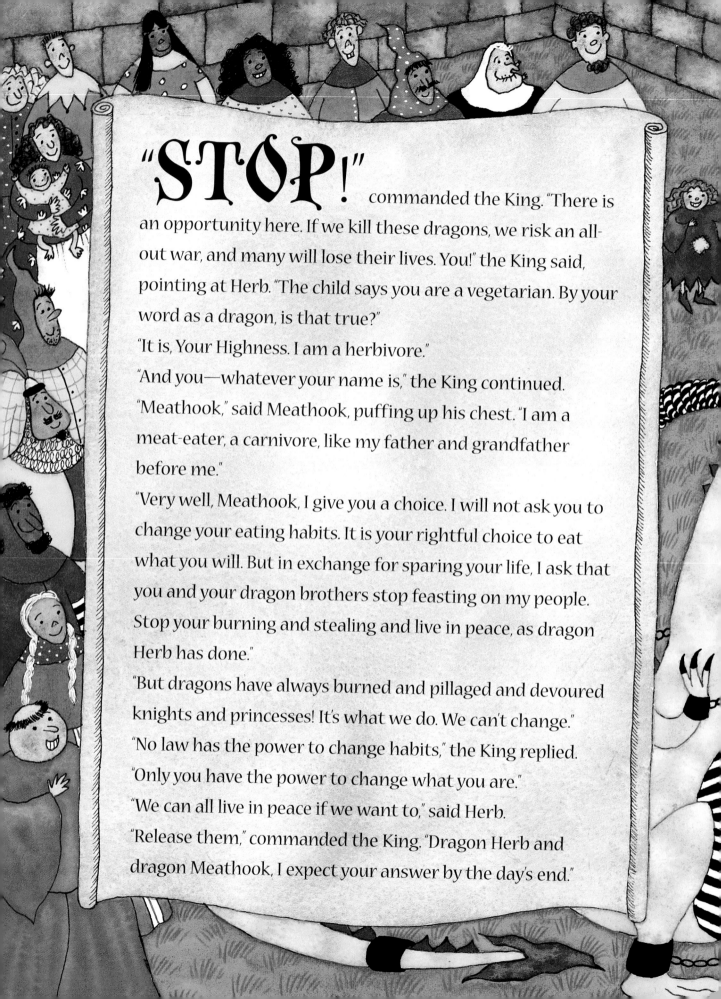

"STOP!"

commanded the King. "There is an opportunity here. If we kill these dragons, we risk an all-out war, and many will lose their lives. You!" the King said, pointing at Herb. "The child says you are a vegetarian. By your word as a dragon, is that true?"

"It is, Your Highness. I am a herbivore."

"And you—whatever your name is," the King continued.

"Meathook," said Meathook, puffing up his chest. "I am a meat-eater, a carnivore, like my father and grandfather before me."

"Very well, Meathook, I give you a choice. I will not ask you to change your eating habits. It is your rightful choice to eat what you will. But in exchange for sparing your life, I ask that you and your dragon brothers stop feasting on my people. Stop your burning and stealing and live in peace, as dragon Herb has done."

"But dragons have always burned and pillaged and devoured knights and princesses! It's what we do. We can't change."

"No law has the power to change habits," the King replied. "Only you have the power to change what you are."

"We can all live in peace if we want to," said Herb.

"Release them," commanded the King. "Dragon Herb and dragon Meathook, I expect your answer by the day's end."

In the hidden cave, all the dragons of Nogard met to hear of the king's offer.

"It's a trick to de-dragon us!" shouted one.

"Better than an endless war, isn't it?" shouted another.

"It's not as if we have to become vegetarians like Herb. We just have to give up eating people," said a large dragon from the rear.

"Live in peace with people? I can't imagine it," said another.

"I wouldn't mind having a nice garden like Herb has," said one of the younger dragons.

"And I'll help you if you like," offered Herb. "I'll give you some seeds and show you how to sow and reap."

"We must vote on it," announced Meathook. "Now!"

Then all of the dragons voted and the result of that vote is recorded in the history books of Nogard. And even to this day, the story is told of how Herb, the vegetarian dragon, brought peace to the forest of Nogard, where dragons and people, meat-eaters and vegetarians, live together in peace and harmony.